Betty Bunny
Loves Chocolate Cake

WRITTEN BY

Michael B. Kaplan

ILLUSTRATED BY

Stéphane Jorisch

Dial Books for Young Readers an imprint of Penguin Group (USA) Inc.

For Will, Kate, and Hank—Betty Bunny's
loving and supportive siblings —M.B.K.

For B., not as in Betty but just like Betty
—S.J.

DIAL BOOKS FOR YOUNG READERS • A division of Penguin Young Readers Group
Published by The Penguin Group • Penguin Group (USA) Inc., 375 Hudson Street, New York, NY 10014, U.S.A. • Penguin Group (Canada), 90 Eglinton
Avenue East, Suite 700, Toronto, Ontario, Canada M4P 2Y3 (a division of Pearson Penguin Canada Inc.) • Penguin Books Ltd, 80 Strand, London WC2R
0RL, England • Penguin Ireland, 25 St. Stephen's Green, Dublin 2, Ireland (a division of Penguin Books Ltd) • Penguin Group (Australia), 250 Camberwell
Road, Camberwell, Victoria 3124, Australia (a division of Pearson Australia Group Pty Ltd) • Penguin Books India Pvt Ltd, 11 Community Centre,
Panchsheel Park, New Delhi - 110 017, India • Penguin Group (NZ), 67 Apollo Drive, Rosedale, North Shore 0632, New Zealand (a division of Pearson
New Zealand Ltd) • Penguin Books (South Africa) (Pty) Ltd, 24 Sturdee Avenue, Rosebank, Johannesburg 2196, South Africa • Penguin Books Ltd,
Registered Offices: 80 Strand, London WC2R 0RL, England

Designed by Jennifer Kelly
Text set in Gararond
Manufactured in China on acid-free paper

10 9 8 7 6 5 4 3

Library of Congress Cataloging-in-Publication Data
Kaplan, Michael B.
Betty Bunny loves chocolate cake / by Michael B. Kaplan ; pictures by Stéphane Jorisch.   p. cm.
Summary: From her first bite, young Betty Bunny likes chocolate cake so much that she claims she will marry it one day, and she has trouble learning to wait
patiently until she can have her next taste.
ISBN 978-0-8037-3407-4 (hardcover)   [1. Patience—Fiction. 2. Behavior—Fiction. 3. Food habits—Fiction. 4. Family life—Fiction. 5. Rabbits—Fiction.
6. Cake—Fiction.] I. Jorisch, Stéphane, ill. II. Title.
PZ7.K12942 Bet 2011   [E]—dc22   2010028799

The artwork is rendered on Lanaquarelle watercolor paper in pencil, ink, watercolor, and gouache.

Betty Bunny was a handful.

She knew this because her mother always said, "Betty Bunny, you are a handful." And her father always said, "Your mother sure is right about that." Betty Bunny knew that her mother and father loved her, and so being a handful must be **very,** **very good.**

One day, after a healthy dinner of carrots, potatoes, and peas, Mother said, "Who wants dessert? I have chocolate cake."

Betty Bunny, who was not very good at trying new things, announced: "I hate chocolate cake. Chocolate cake is yucky.

What's chocolate cake?"

So her mother gave her a piece. And Betty Bunny tried it. It was the yummiest thing she had ever put in her mouth.

"When I grow up, I am going to marry chocolate cake!" said Betty Bunny.

"You can't marry a dessert," said her brother Henry.

"You could marry a baker who *makes* chocolate cake," added her sister Kate.

"Or you could just buy your cake at the store, and then you don't have to marry anyone," said their older brother Bill.

Betty Bunny thought about it for a while.
"No," she finally said. "I am going to marry
chocolate cake."

"Whatever," said Bill. "But you're going to
have really weird-looking kids."

That night, Betty Bunny's mother kissed her and tucked her in. "Good night, Betty Bunny. I love you," she said.

Betty Bunny looked up into her mother's eyes and said, "Good night, Mommy. I love chocolate cake."

The next day at school, Betty Bunny's teacher said, "Good morning, Betty Bunny, how are you?"

Betty Bunny said, "I'm a handful and I love chocolate cake."

Her teacher said, "**A** is for apple,

B is for ball,

C is for cat. "

Betty Bunny said, "**A** is for chocolate cake,

B is for chocolate cake,

C is for **chocolate cake.**"

During playground time, Betty Bunny tried to make chocolate cake by mixing water and dirt.

It looked a little like chocolate cake.

But it didn't taste very much like chocolate cake. Betty Bunny started to cry.

"**I want chocolate cake,**" she said.

Her teacher told her that they had no chocolate cake at school. Betty Bunny said, "I hate school. School is **yucky.**"

After school, her mother drove her home. "How was your day?" she asked.

"I ate mud," Betty Bunny answered unhappily. "I want chocolate cake."

"Sometimes," her mother explained, "you can't have what you want right away, so you need to wait. And that's called having patience."

"But I don't want to have patience," Betty Bunny protested. **"I want to have chocolate cake."**

That night at dinner, her mother told Betty Bunny she could not have dessert until she ate a healthy dinner. Usually, Betty Bunny liked healthy food. Not tonight. Tonight, all she wanted was chocolate cake. Her father told her, "Don't come to me hoping to get a different answer."

Henry said,
"If you were smart,
you'd eat some peas."

Kate said, "You should try some carrots.
They make cake out of them too, you know."

Bill said, "Why don't you have
some chocolate cake? That's what
you really want. Oh, no, wait. You
can't. Ha-ha."

Betty Bunny picked up some peas. She threw them at Henry.

She threw some carrots at Kate.

And, worst of all, she threw mashed potatoes at Bill. They stuck to his forehead.

Everyone was shocked. Even Betty Bunny was shocked.

She hadn't really meant to do something so awful.

Mother was not happy that Bill had teased his sister. She was even less happy with Betty Bunny. She told Betty Bunny to go straight to bed. There would be no chocolate cake tonight. Betty Bunny screamed, **"This family is yucky!"**

Then she remembered she was hungry. So she crammed her mouth full of peas, carrots, and mashed potatoes and ran off to bed.

When her mother came into her room to kiss her good night, she told Betty Bunny: "Sweetheart, you know that I still love you."

"Mommy," Betty Bunny said, "you know that I still love chocolate cake."

Just thinking about the cake she was not eating made her cry.
Then it made her scream. Then it made her kick the wall.
Which hurt her foot. Which made her cry all over again.

"Betty Bunny," her mother said as she rubbed the little bunny's foot, "I am going to put a piece of chocolate cake on a plate in the refrigerator. It will be your piece of cake. And you can eat it tomorrow after a healthy dinner. Maybe if you know it's there waiting for you, it will be easier to be patient."

Betty Bunny stopped crying. She liked this idea, so she wanted to say something especially nice to her mother. "Mommy," she said, "you are a handful."

The next morning, Betty Bunny wanted to say good-bye to her chocolate cake before she left for school. So she opened the refrigerator and saw her piece of cake sitting on its plate. It looked so lonely.

Betty Bunny knew that the cake would miss her all day while she was at school.

So she picked it up and put it in her pocket.

At school, her teacher said, "Betty Bunny, you seem very happy today."
Betty Bunny just giggled. There was chocolate cake in her pocket, and
no one knew it but her.

As Betty Bunny finished munching her last carrot at dinner that night, her mother smiled. "Betty Bunny," she said, "you were patient and waited all day for your cake. You ate a good dinner. I am very proud of you. Would you like to get out your cake now?"

Betty Bunny reached into her pocket. Her cake was gone! Instead of cake, her pocket was filled with a **brown,**

goopy
mess.

"My cake!"

Henry said, "I can't believe you put cake in your pocket."

Kate said, "Betty Bunny, food doesn't go in your pocket."

Bill said, "Guess you can't marry that piece of cake *now*."

Her mother got her a new piece of cake, and she explained that putting cake in your pocket is not really the same as being patient. Betty Bunny finally understood. She promised from now on she would be patient.